One Night Changed Everything

By: Mary Whitney

Prologue

Emma's POV

All I was doing was merely giving a fellow hotel guest

directions on how to get to the local bus station since I

know the area so well and because I'm a decent human

being unlike most people these days. What I didn't realize

right away though was that the hotel guest was having a

couple's spat with his girlfriend (or now ex-girlfriend?) and she nearly ran me down with her car out of jealousy, not once... but twice. The "excitement" caused Jason to shoot right up from his office chair behind the front desk and storm outside. He immediately started interrogating both guests before ushering me back inside after a mild outburst slipped out of my mouth. If looks could kill, his easily would have done so to me. His facial expression definitely pierced my heart in that moment. That facial expression he displayed to me is one that I hope to never see again.

I've liked Jason for a long time now and I was making such great progress with him in the flirting department…up until tonight that is. Up until tonight, he was actually considering going out with me on his day off next week. Now because of an event that was out of my control, an event that caused my anxiety to flare up, he's being cold to me. Instead of fleeing the lobby like I wanted to (and logically should have) when the male hotel guest came back a second time, my anxiety got the best of me and caused me to freeze up. *Sighs* What I wouldn't give to redo the events of the past twenty four hours and pretend that they never happened... I so badly want to move past this rough patch with Jason, but the question is, does he? I truly don't know...

Chapter 1

Emma's POV

I'm heading to Virginia Beach for a long weekend getaway. Hotels just began to reopen recently along with many other places that were closed for months due to the coronavirus pandemic. Also, the summer rates really kick into gear next week so after this stay, I'll have to take a break for a little while or else my bank account will hate me. Virginia Beach is my happy place, a place that I absolutely could refer to as home permanently one day. I've also had a certain someone on the brain lately, someone that I've made really good progress with in the flirting department, that being my long time crush Jason Langford. He's the assistant manager at my favorite hotel in Virginia Beach.

I've liked him for years but when I first liked him way back when, I was too young for him and I understood because truthfully I was too young despite being of legal age. Now though, I'm 25 and am getting to the age where I'm ready for a serious relationship. I'm tired of people wasting my time. Jason is quite a bit older than me, fifteen years my senior which translates to him being 40. Him and

I have been close friends for four years now, but back in May when the hotel was still closed due to pandemic restrictions/regulations, my father and I came down to visit. The visit went well, lasting for an entire hour despite him being busy with renovations along with the rest of the staff. During this visit, my father inquired deeper into what Jason really thinks of me... and it turns out that he FINALLY likes me back! I couldn't believe my ears when he told me that. I've been jumping for joy ever since to be honest.

I finally got Jason's cell phone number a couple weeks ago from Gibson (the hotel general manager who my parents and I are good friends with) and we've been talking frequently since. Jason is a slender man, his height is approximately 5'11. He's tall but not a giant, which is kind of a relief because massively tall people intimidate me. His hair is black with a few grey hairs beginning to appear a bit early (it suits him though). As we approach the outskirts of Virginia Beach, I become giddy. Jason consumes my thoughts. As stupid as this may sound, I decided to dress up a bit to impress him. Not anything grand, but I'm supporting a new black and white jumpsuit that I bought at Target recently. It has a bow in the middle of it and it's super cute.

A half an hour later...

My parents and I are about to approach the entrance to the hotel's parking lot. (I'm riding shotgun up front to be the eyes for my dad in the dark in case he needs me to provide him with any additional guidance on where to park and what not (my parents and I take turns driving on trips though). Jason and I immediately make eye contact through the window and he comes rushing out to help us carry in our bags before checking us in. He then carries most of our bags down the hallway to our room. We always stay in a first floor room because my dad is older and handicapped to some degree. He walks with one cane but may need to start using a second one soon. Jason then proceeded to tease me about paying seven hundred dollars for our stay when in reality it only cost me three hundred dollars. I plop down onto the bed and sigh contently as soon as I'm settled into the room. I've missed this place so much, this bed included. The new mattresses the owner got during the winter are marvelous, so much more comfortable than the old ones.

The weather is warmer now but thankfully it isn't the fourth of July yet. Quite frankly, I wouldn't want to be here on the fourth of July. The crowds are too large, the partying is nonstop, all you hear is fireworks constantly every night, etc. I can't wait to see what this stay brings!

Chapter 2

Jason's POV

I've secretly liked Emma for two years now but because she's quite a bit younger than me, I've been hesitant to act on my feelings for her. When her father approached me about the subject back in May, it certainly surprised me. I knew she liked me back then but I rejected her to protect the both of us. I didn't want to hurt her in any way (but I obviously did) but I also was selfish, I didn't want to ruin my image/reputation at my best job yet. I'm forty and though I'm not ancient, I'm certainly not getting any younger either. I really do like her though but I don't want to rush things between us. I want to continue being close friends... but yet maybe flirt a little and see how that goes.

She's currently hanging out in the lobby with me while I'm running around like a chicken with my head cut off. I chat with her during the lull periods and she does some computer work whenever I'm busy to occupy herself. Emma sitting in her lavender colored dress is such a lovely slight, so pleasant on the eyes. She's even showing more leg than usual and I made sure to tease her about it, causing her to blush twice. When I'm down carrying some luggage up to the second floor, I smirk at her. "So what time are you staying until?" She mirrors my smirk. "Until eleven." I blush while continuing to smirk at her. "That's when I get off of work." She rolls her eyes playfully. "I know." Emma blushes and crosses one leg over the other.

We then find ourselves chatting about different kinds of phone wallpaper of all topics. I show her this app with these space/galaxy themed ones that I think she'd like. She nods in approval at every single one of them. This then leads to me recommending her a puzzle app game that's only a dollar to buy in the app store. It's called "The Room." It has the highest ratings out of all of the puzzle games in the Google Play app store and a lot of positive feedback. She doesn't like to pay for apps but says she'll keep it in mind. I end up playing a few rounds of it while chatting with her to keep up with my elite player status. Later on, I find myself wanting to impress her a bit by showing her my latest work-out regimen (making sure to do so when it's just the two of us alone in the lobby. Being trampled by other hotel guests would be both awkward and painful). I do fifty push-ups, ten lunges, hand weight lifting behind the desk, stretches, and more.

Emma then takes me by surprise and does some push-ups herself. She isn't as skilled at them as I am but I appreciate the effort. Emma is a healthy weight but sure does have some nice curves. I try my best not to look at her ass when it's hoisted up in front of my face but I can't help it, it's literally right in front of my face. When I'm behind the desk, I do my best to calm down the woody that formed inside my pants rather quickly. I definitely don't need any guests or co-workers to notice it… Damn it Emma, she shouldn't do this to me while I'm at work. When I'm in assistant manager mode, I can't say or do half of the things with her that I'd like to. Gibson lives in an apartment attached to the hotel and makes random appearances along with the owner. The owner's name is Marshall and he can be a hard ass at times. Marshall runs a tight ship and doesn't trust others easily, but he trusts me a lot surprisingly. I don't want to do anything rash to breach that threshold of trust. I've been working here for nearly six years now, five of which I've spent being assistant manager.

Does this job have some headaches? Yes, absolutely. The thing is, I made some mistakes in the past in my teaching career that got me fired and Marshall gave me a second chance, unlike most people. The other businesses I interviewed with treated me rather strangely and/or basically rejected me on the spot. I even applied for two more teaching positions in the area and got turned down for both of them. It stinks but oh well, it is what it is. I do like the hotel industry a lot and can picture myself eventually being general manager at either this property or one similar to it.

The evening flies by rather quickly and it is eleven o'clock before we both know it. I let Emma stall for an extra ten minutes due to a late check in but I'm sad to see her have to leave, even though I know we'll be back at it again tomorrow. I give her a gentle pat on the back and bid her "Good night" before watching her head back to her room down the hall. I think to myself "My God, Emma is stunning." It even takes me a minute to snap out of my trance and lock up the lobby for the night.

Chapter 3

Emma's POV

Time Skip... The Next Morning...

I head to breakfast in the pool area with some extra pep in my step. Last night's hang out session in the lobby with Jason was stellar. I'm so proud of the progress that I've made with him. My parents are both teasing me as I devour my everything bagel with butter over it. My dad wiggles his eyebrows at me every time one of the workers on duty mentions Jason and I'm trying not to blush, making it obvious to everyone that I have the hots for the assistant manager of the establishment. "Daaaadddd", I whine loudly. "Can you not make such a big deal out of this?" He laughs before smiling sincerely. "I'm sorry Emma, I just know you've liked him for so long now and now that he finally reciprocates those feelings on a deeper level, I really want this to work out for you. If it doesn't, I'll kick his ass for you. I may be elderly but my canes have other purposes too."

I giggle but my expression softens at his sincerity. "Thank you Dad, I love you so much. I hope you know that." He puts a hand over his heart. "I do indeed but it feels good hearing the words said aloud." My mom nods in agreement. "Your father isn't perfect honey but when it comes to you, he would literally fight to the death in your honor. I'd do the exact same for you. I love you too, to infinity and beyond." I giggle internally at the Toy Story reference but my heart is melting at their kindness. Seriously, I'm so blessed to have two wonderful parents like mine. So many people take that for granted and/or don't appreciate their parents enough, which is devastating (especially in the long run).

We spend the latter part of the morning walking around on the main street, browsing in the shops and breathing in the ocean air. We all cherish breathing in the ocean air whenever we're here, especially my dad. If he won the lottery, I know he'd buy a house near the ocean the very next day. I probably would do the same. I love this area so much, I'd give a lot to be able to live here one day. It isn't cheap but then again what is these days, you know? Rent, mortgages, etc cost an arm and a leg in most places all across the country (and around the world even). We then go to the large shopping mall that many of the locals depend on for most of their shopping, entertainment, etc. I may be twenty five years old but Rue21 is still one of my favorite stores. Being such an avid reader, I could practically live in the Barnes and Noble in the mall. Sipping a Chai Latte while reading a good book or magazine is pure bliss for me.

We then of course end the day down at the beach. My parents and I sit on a beach overlooking the ocean for about two hours before we finally force ourselves to head back to the hotel for the night. Upon our arrival, Jason is standing outside vaping. I'm not keen on vaping but it's not as harmful as smoking. Hopefully he'll stop smoking all together one day though... I beam at him. "Hey Jason. Does Gibson know you're vaping?" He nearly jumps and it causes me to burst into laughter. "Emma, you know how I feel about you doing that to me. One day you'll do it and Gibson will actually be standing behind me. I could get into trouble for vaping while on the job, well with the exception of my rare break periods." I laugh once more. "I know, I'm sorry. I promise you that my parents and I, well mainly myself, do it to you out of love." He huffs. "Whatever you say Emma. I can tell you obviously went shopping today so let me help you carry in some of the bags. Let me guess, you got another new bathing suit."

I smirk at him. "Maybe, maybe not. I'll leave that to your imagination. If I did, I'll be sure to sport it in the near future. Some of my swimsuits are more on the simple side and yet I still get harassed by men in the hot tub." He grimaces. "I know, you've been harassed by some real winners these past few months." I nod. "The worst experience was the drunk couple that wanted me to have a threesome with them." Jason winces. "No kidding. The woman even asked myself and the pool attendant on duty that night if we had any lubricant for them to have intercourse with. Thank goodness you didn't go out with them for karaoke down the street. If anything bad were to happen to you, I'd never forgive myself." My smirk softens into a shy smile. "Really?" He looks at me seriously. "Really." The mood shifts back and forth between playful and serious between us for the rest of the day. We're both getting to the other, causing an array of emotions to float to the surface.

Chapter 4

Jason's POV

Time Skip... The Next Day... Suppertime...

It's about six thirty in the evening when Emma comes back from one of her usual walks around the neighborhood. Despite her having earbuds in her ears to listen to music with, she's typically very alert of her surroundings. The only issue is her appearance... don't get me wrong she looks beautiful, but a little too glammed up for a mere stroll around the block. She's wearing a new dress (I have an excellent memory and I know for certain that I've never seen her wear it before) that shows quite a bit of her back and a little cleavage. There's a guy that approaches her out of nowhere and I can feel my inner Hulk wanting to lunge at him instantly. I want to fight him over a girl that isn't even officially mine...

He reminds me one of those guys in a punk rock band. I mean I should know, I've listened to a lot of punk rock music over the years. From what little I can hear of the conversation, Emma is giving him instructions on how to get to the local bus station. The commotion that follows is what really puts me on edge. The guy's current girlfriend makes the assumption that he's going out with Emma now out of spite to make her jealous and she nearly hits Emma with her car... not once, but twice... Several guests are staring wide eyed at the scene on display before us. Now I'm really starting to get upset. I gently grab a hold of Emma and bring her into the lobby. I run a hand through my hair in frustration. "Emma, I need you to tell me exactly what happened out there that has caused you to become so distraught. I need to know whether or not I have to throw those guests out and call the police."

Emma tells me the complete story, every single detail. My heart is doing flips and so is my stomach while she tells me everything. Emma didn't do anything wrong but she also trusted that guy too easily. She trusts more easily than I do, but I can't judge too harshly because I wasn't the one in that situation, she was. Based on everything that she has told me, I know exactly what to say next. She's not going to like it but it has to be said. "Emma, I need you to listen to me very carefully because I'm only going to say what I'm about to say once because I need to get this situation under control before Gibson or the owner finds out about what's going on. I need you to head back to your room and talk with your parents about what happened. Technically that woman trying to run you down is attempted assault and battery. It's up to you whether or not you want to take legal action against her. I'm going to monitor the lobby in addition to checking out that guy's room in the other building. Do not come until the coast is clear. That's not a request, it's an order. Do you understand?"

With tears in her eyes and a heavy heart, she leaves without saying another word. Usually she objects to my occasional bossy demeanor but she's so upset that doesn't bother objecting to my orders. That's how I know that this is very serious... The next hour is the most stressful hour I've endured at work in a while. The guy goes back and forth between the lobby and his room twice before he leaves to who knows where. A half an hour after that, Emma appears once again. Her eyes are bloodshot and she's still sniffling. I'm pretty sure I heard her vomiting a couple of times. I'm heartbroken for her, I'm heartbroken that I have to be cold. "Emma, I don't know where he is."

She sighs. "I-I figured. I just wanted to make sure you

were okay." I sigh back. "I'm fine but I'm not much in the

mood for socializing right now. You're welcome to stay

but he if comes back, please leave."

She nods and does some adult coloring to soothe her

stress a bit. When the guy appears again about forty five

minutes later, shit is indeed about to hit the fan. Emma

tries to force herself to leave but fails to do so. The guy is

now drunk off his ass and is ranting to me about his now

ex-girlfriend. He even gives a speech on how a real woman

is one like Emma, one that would spend hours sitting in a

hotel lobby while I'm on the clock just to get the chance to

chat with me, even if it's just for a few minutes. He's not

wrong about Emma being a real woman but he's definitely

striking a nerve by talking about her in that limelight,

especially when he's a stranger both to her and in general.

Something inside me snaps and I look him dead in the eyes and say "You have twenty minutes to pack your things and vacate the property. If you're not gone in twenty minutes, I'm calling the cops." He looks at me in disbelief when he finally realizes that I'm not bluffing about a minute later and begins stumbling towards his room.

When he's out of earshot, I get all up in her face. "EMMA! SERIOUSLY? WHY DIDN'T YOU LEAVE?" She stands there in shock. "I-I don't know. I-I wanted to but my body wouldn't let me." I know that she has struggled with anxiety for years now but I'm just so frustrated that my anger won't let me take that into consideration at the moment. Emma and I have a stare down before she willingly leaves this time. Will she come back a third time? Who knows, I've probably just shattered her heart, which is the one thing I was hoping to avoid in the progress that I've been making with her romantically.

I'm pretty sure that has gone down the tubes now... Story

of my life...

Chapter 5

Emma's POV

  I CAN'T BELIEVE HE THINKS THAT I WOULD

WILLINGLY SUBMIT MYSELF TO THAT!!! Why

would I willingly submit myself to harassment from

strangers? Why would I purposely want my anxiety to get

the best of me and make me act like a completely different

person, not myself? I have so many questions right now

and hardly have received any answers to them. Does Jason

still care about me? Does he hate me or just merely dislike

me at the moment? Neither option is a pleasant thought. I'm so upset, I was making such great progress with Jason. The feelings I had hoped he would reciprocate for years for me finally floated to the surface recently and I was foolish enough to think that things between us would blossom. I'm an idiot, the biggest idiot on the face of the Earth. Well, maybe not on the entire face of the Earth but still a decent sized idiot.

Do you really want to know just how idiotic I am? Maybe you do and maybe you don't, but I'm going to tell you anyways because I really need to vent. Right before I turned back to head to my room in silence once and for all tonight, I paused in the vending machine area adjacent to the lobby. It's tucked away in a corner right before the lobby and stairs leading down to this strip of rooms. I stood there quietly for about ten minutes, pretending to mull over snack options but in reality was eavesdropping on a rather private conversation between Jason and one of the new hire girls. I think she's going to be both a pool attendant and housekeeper. Anyways, that's not the point. What the point is though, is that she flat out asked him if was single and he bragged to her about his bachelor status. He didn't mention that already was interested in someone but hadn't officially asked them out just yet (that someone being me obviously).

I saw her pull on his tie a bit (something I've gotten away with a few times)... and he didn't stop her. That's when my heart really sank into the pits of my stomach. I've never felt more humiliated by a guy than I have in that moment, which is saying a lot because I've dated other staff members at this very hotel, though they shall not be named because they aren't worth that "honor." I'm going to be known as the 'hotel jinx' every time I stay here from here on and out, I feel it in my gut… and it sucks. I've loved the hotel itself for years and I don't want a bad experience with a guy to ruin this place I love. The previous partners did their damage to me but this horrible night with Jason is the last straw. I'm never dating anyone who works at this hotel ever again. Not only am I waving the white flag of surrender, but I'm coming to a crucial realization. I can't be with someone who doesn't know what they want... or more importantly, who they want. I deserve better than to be someone's side piece…

I want someone who truly wants me, someone who won't run every time things get slightly dark. I want someone who is in the relationship with me for the long haul. Someone who can actually picture having a future with me and vice versa. I'm twenty five years old and I'm not getting any younger. In fact, I'm getting older and the simple truth is I'm way past done with these middle and high school games. Jason is playing a childish game with both myself and my feelings for him. I DON'T WANT TO PLAY ANYMORE!!!! My parents both continue to look at me with concern quite evident on their faces. My mother is doing a majority of the talking to comfort me though. "Emma, do you know what you'll do about this?" I nod weakly. "I-I do." She looks at me seriously. "What are you going to do? How are you going to move forward?"

I take a shaky breath, look her right in the eyes, and say "I'm moving on." I have to take a moment to process these words before I continue speaking. "Jason clearly doesn't value me as much as I thought he did, not even as a friend. What really stinks about this situation is not only is my romantic progress with him ruined, but I also lost a close friend. We've built an overall rock solid friendship over the past four years. I was almost certain he'd continue to be in my life but this is turning point. Like you've told me many times over the course of my life, some things eventually change, either for the better or for the worse.

Though this seems like it's changing for the worst, I know

that in the long run it'll be for the better. I'll be the better

for moving on and letting of a person who doesn't value

me nor can they commit to anyone but themselves. I

deserve better than that, I really do."

My mom motions me over to her bedside and pulls me

into a warm embrace, kissing me on the forehead too. "I'm

so proud of you and am always in awe of your strength. I

have no doubt in my mind that you won't be okay. Maybe

not tomorrow, but eventually, you will be. I love you so

much Emma. You're a shining star and I don't ever want to

see anyone attempt to take your shine away. Okay?" I nod

with a sad smile. "I love you too Mom and okay." My dad

mutters something in his sleep. I think it was something

along the lines of "That's my girl", which honestly warms

my heart. For the first time tonight, I do believe that I

eventually be okay. I may need to cry my feelings out a few more times, but I will reach that better place mentally and emotionally eventually.

Chapter 6

Jason's POV

I've really dug myself even deeper into the current hole that I'm in. Not only am I extremely on edge because that sketchy guy is still staying here for the night, but I ruined my chances at a potential date with the new pool attendant/housekeeper. Her name is Melinda and she's only two years older than Emma, making her twenty-seven years old. She's really cute and since my chances with

Emma are toast, I didn't want to dwell over the loss for long... but yet... I feel like absolute shit. I have liked Emma for a long time and having hit on Melinda makes me feel like I've betrayed her, big time. Let me be honest, I definitely did. There's no rectifying my bond with Emma, it's over. From here on out, I'm just a hotel clerk and she's a guest. Nothing more, nothing less.

As I head out to my car, I can sense someone's presence in close proximity to me. I walk a few more steps before I see a shadow reflect off of one of the buildings under the streetlamps. I reluctantly turn around and I'm face to face with the asshole who I so badly wish had been taken away by the cops. As badly I wanted the police to deal with him rather than myself any further, I didn't want the hotel to receive any bad publicity. It's bad enough that I had to fill Gibson in on what happened, but thankfully Gibson and I agreed to keep this incident just between us. We really don't need this incident getting back to the owner...

The asshole glares at me. "I accept that I have to leave in the morning. I'll be gone as soon as the sun begins to rise. What I'm struggling to accept is how you let a woman like that one in the lobby walk out of your life. From what she told me earlier, you two seemed very close and you're making a big mistake. I may be drunk off my ass, but I'm still sober enough to recognize a quality woman when I see one." With that being said, he stumbles back to his room and I unlock my chair. As soon as I climb into the driver's side, I slam my head down on the steering wheel in frustration. As much as I hate agreeing with a drunk guy, he's right. I've screwed up big time with Emma. Emma really is a quality woman and not many women like her exist these days. This is one of the biggest screw ups I've ever made…

The drive home only takes me ten minutes since there is no traffic on the roads at this time of night and yet for the entire duration of those ten minutes, I'm having to blink back tears of anguish. Facing Emma from here on out is going to be difficult. She's bound to get hit on again by other guests and/or staff members. Having to silently watch someone else win over her heart just may shatter mine completely. I'm not expecting anyone to pity me (though it would be nice if at least one person did), I did this to myself. Instead of taking the time to understand Emma and remember that she suffers from anxiety flares up at times, I judged her for her actions immediately. I made her look like the villain tonight when in reality she was merely the victim. I'm the true villain in this story. Believe or not, that drunk idiot isn't even the real villain. He didn't cause any harm to Emma, his crazy now ex-girlfriend was the one who tried to run her down with her car, not him.

When I get home, I force myself to take a quick shower. I scrub various parts of my body like hell to get rid of the heaping amount of germs I've most likely contracted today, to try to erase what happened tonight as much as I possibly can. The warm water gives my joints some much needed relief. I must have walked at least ten minutes on property at work today. I hardly sat down because I was so on edge. I then do something incredibly irresponsible. I chug down three cans of beer despite having made it a rule to only drink on my days off. I'm too depressed to give a shit about potentially having a hangover tomorrow.

Chapter 7

The next morning...

I don't say a word to any hotel staff members because I'm quite frankly not in the mood too. I can practically feel Gibson's eyes on me throughout breakfast. When the owner comes around, Gibson puts on a fake happy face to please both him and other guests but as soon as he's out of sight, Gibson is back to staring at me a bit too intensely. I guess he too believes that I've become the hotel jinx after all. I feel even more disappointment about the events of last night than ever before. Jason is off today but he'll back tomorrow, which means I still have to face him for an entire day before I finally get to leave myself. I never thought I'd want to rush a getaway... but I can't wait for it to end. I need some time away from this place, which again is another thing that I never thought that I would say.

I'm at a mental crossroads about whether or not to ever return to this hotel again. My parents love this place and it's the most decent affordable hotel in Virginia Beach. Maybe if I stay away for a couple of months, I'll be over Jason by that point and can have the courage to return here. I know for a fact that my feelings for him won't just disappear overnight, but I also know that I'm not one to stay stuck on someone forever. I've made that mistake as a teenager before and I refuse to make it in adulthood. After breakfast, I decide to apply a light layer of makeup to make myself look a little more presentable... and also to hide the obvious dark circles under my eyes from my lack of sleep. My parents and I had a beach day planned for today and I don't want to disappoint them. Disappointing

my parents is one of the worst feelings.

 After I'm finished getting ready, we all head out to the

car. I help my parents load in a few beach supplies, which

includes towels and a couple of books. I actually want to

dip my toes in the sand today and feel the waves brush up

against my feet. Water therapy is one of the most

beneficial kinds of therapy. My dad knows that just as

much as I do, if not more so. Whenever one of us is

stressed to the max, we almost immediately plan a water

therapy retreat together. It isn't always to the ocean, but

sometimes a local lake or waterfall. Most bodies of water

are therapeutic for us (swamps don't count though).

Swamps tend to smell disgusting, which is not exactly the

definition of therapeutic. More like the recipe for nausea if

you ask me...

The drive to the beach takes about fifteen minutes without stops... though we did stop for ice cream at Dairy Queen on the way since it's lunch time now and they open at eleven. My mom and I help my dad over to a bench. He's content on the beach immediately. We sit with him for a bit while eating our ice creams before I decide to move on down to the beach itself for some alone time (I don't get a lot of it). I brought two books with me today, one of which I'm almost finished with and a second one to start on. The one I'm almost finished with is a Nicholas Sparks romance novel that has hit me in my feels as does all of his books that I read do and the other is the Hunger Games prequel book that I've heard a lot of hype about. I used to be really into that trilogy awhile back so I figured why not read this book too. It'll be interesting to learn about what President Snow was like in his younger years.

As soon as I dig my feet into the wet sand and the waves gently brush up against me, I instantly feel more relaxed. Don't worry, I'm being absolutely careful with my books. I have yet to ever drop a book into the ocean and I don't plan on starting to do so today. This beach day is exactly what we all needed, especially me to be honest. For the most part, Jason doesn't pop into my mind too much. I'm extremely grateful for that because one of the main reasons for this beach day was to distract myself, to make myself feel better, even just temporarily. Well guess what, mission accomplished. I really do feel better by being here, disconnecting from the rest of society for a little while. Jason who?

Chapter 8

Jason's POV

Today is my one day off of the week and honestly, it couldn't have come a better time. There is no way I would be able to be in the same room as Emma for longer than necessary. I definitely wouldn't be able to look her in the eyes. I know I'll have to tomorrow but at least I have a day to prepare myself for the inevitable reality of tomorrow, in which I actually have to face her again in person. I know for a fact that's it's going to be awkward, but I'm really hoping it isn't too tense. Work is tense enough for me at times as is, I don't need Emma to increase that tension (especially not on purpose). She's more vocal about her thoughts and feelings than I am, but she also has a bit of a temper. She lashed out once at one other staff member who she had a brief fling with after she found out that he was already seeing someone and just wasting her time because she's a beautiful young lady. It wasn't pretty... at all...

I'm currently visiting my mother as I do every day and she's seizing me up a bit. She's my mother, she knows me better than everyone. She can tell that I'm not acting like myself, clearly. "Jason, what's bothering you?" I look at her with tired eyes. "I messed up big time with a girl I really like...I mean liked." She raises an eyebrow. "What'd you do?" I go into complete detail about the incident that occurred hotel last night. My mother nods along and patiently listens to everything I have to say before she speaks. "Jason, I can understand both sides of this issue. I understand that you didn't want your job to be jeopardized. I know the guy you work for isn't the easiest man in the world to work for and your current job is the best one you've had in years. As for this Emma girl, it wasn't her fault. She struggles with anxiety and made it clear to you several times that she does indeed suffer from it. Instead of being sympathetic and trying to understand her, you judged her and only cared about yourself in the moment. I know the truth is harsh sometimes, but you need to hear it son."

I hang my head down in shame but I don't argue against that claim because she's right. I did hurt Emma, severely. I should have been more sympathetic to Emma and I wasn't. "One more thing son. You never and I mean never, hit on another woman when the woman you are with and/or had planned on being with is right within earshot of you. From what you told me, she was standing just around the corner and heard every word of you hitting on that new employee. Jason, you're better than this. After that one entanglement with that former Russian girl who used to work in housekeeping, you vowed not only to me but to yourself that you would never date another co-worker again. You got caught up with the wrong woman and she took you for a ride. The right woman is right in front of you and you just let her walk away. Mixing business with pleasure rarely ever works out for anyone. Also, Emma sounds like a wonderful person and I feel for that poor girl, she's probably so heartbroken because of your ignorant actions."

A tear slips down my cheek. "Mom, I know I messed up. I realized so last night right before I clocked out of work, but the damage has already been done. I don't know if I can reconcile even a friendship with her. Yes it's better that she's a guest rather than an employee... but who knows if she'll even ever want to return back to this hotel again after the end of her stay. Tomorrow is her last night at the hotel and I know she won't want to speak to me." She puts a hand on my shoulder and rubs it gently. "You don't know unless you try. It's better to try and to fail than to not try

and forever wonder what could have been. Right?" I sigh.
"Sometimes I hate it when you're right, but thank you for listening to me vent Mom. I love you and have enjoyed our visit today, like I do all of our visits." She hugs me gently and kisses me on the cheek. "I love you too son. Keep me posted on how tomorrow goes. Take care and don't overdo it today, it's your only day off of the week."

I nod. "Will do Mom." I use the bathroom real quick, wash my hand, and then begin heading out to run some errands like grocery shopping, getting gas, going to the bank, etc. Throughout the entire day, the anxiety of seeing Emma tomorrow looms over me like a dark cloud. I'm really dreading tomorrow but at the same time, I just want to get it over with. Wish me luck, I'll certainly need it...

Chapter 9

Emma's POV

Time Skip... The Next Day...

It's currently late morning, about eleven thirty to be exact. Today is my final full day down here during this stay and so much is running through my mind, as is the list of things I want to do today. At the top of that list, it includes staying away from Jason as much as I possibly can. If I catch him looking at me, I will immediately turn my back to him. I refuse to give him any attention, he's not worth my time and energy. My parents are both excited about getting to go to the beach again today and I don't want to diminish their excitement with my anxiety...

I finish throwing on a cute outfit (my mom thought it would a good idea to doll myself up, a way to lift my spirits). As I look at my reflection in the mirror, I do agree with her. I do feel both a little more uplifted and look better in general today. The color has returned to my skin, I'm nowhere near as pale as I was even yesterday. Not even Gibson's questioning looks will have power over me today. Let people talk about me as much as they please. The more they talk about me, the more important I must be, right? That's what many celebrities say when rumors get spread about them and a lot of the public is dumb enough to buy into said rumors. I even tie a ribbon into my hair to give my outfit some extra flare. The dress is purple and the ribbon is pink, purple and pink being two colors that go well together.

For shoes, I throw on some comfortable black sandals with a silver, kind of swirly lining on the bottom of each one. I take a vitamin, brush my teeth, and floss. I decide to bail on makeup today though. Too much makeup application on your skin only does more harm than good in the long run. I have enough patches of acne as is, I don't need anymore. I then gather the things that I actually need for today, switch the sign on the door to "Please make up room", and make sure the door is locked behind me. Both of my parents are patiently waiting out in the car, sipping on hot cups of coffee. I giggle to myself, my parents are both coffee addicts, especially my mom. My dad can handle going without coffee for a few days, but not my mom. I'm like that too but with tea rather than coffee. Both the taste and smell of coffee makes me nauseated.

I skipped breakfast today so the first thing we do is stop for me to grab some lunch at Wendy's. I opt for some chili and fries (separately). The wait in the drive thru is short so I get my food in like ten minutes. We then park so

I can eat before we head down to our next destination, the beach. The first thing I notice when we get to the beach is that there's more wave action today than there was yesterday. That makes my dad giddy and he rushes out to the bench to sit in excitement. We also can smell the ocean a bit more today. Some people don't like the smell of the ocean but we all personally love it. Jason is completely forgotten about yet again... for now...

That evening...

When we get back from our rather adventurous day that did indeed include a bit more shopping at one of the local gift shops down the street from the hotel, Jason is standing right outside one of the doors vaping. There's no one else around besides him. We unfortunately make eye contact for a moment and we both tense up. I don't say anything and neither does he. We just stare at each other, my gaze hardening more with each passing second that we look at each other. Neither one of us actually breaks the silence though because despite his actions, he does have at least one brain cell left to tell him that speaking to me isn't a good idea right now, especially if it doesn't concern hotel matters. My mom notices Jason staring at me after a full minute and makes a face at him that screams "Leave us alone", which is enough to cause him to hurry back inside and man the desk, where he belongs.

I silently thank my Mom as we all head inside, my dad lingering in the car for a bit because he wants to catch the weather forecast for next week on the radio. I knew with my crappy luck that I was going to run into Jason as soon as I came back today. What makes matters worse though is that he looms over me all evening off and on while I'm trying to enjoy myself in the pool area. I make small talk with strangers whenever my parents step away just so I don't have any reason to even so much as look at him again. I can hear him sigh audibly whenever I do that. Good jerk wad, sigh all you want. You can sigh until the cows come home and I still won't be speaking to you unless it involves a hotel matter that you actually have to attend to.

I apologize, I'm ranting again. Some people just irk me so much, especially those that start out as decent human beings and then they reveal their true colors, showing how lousy of human beings they actually are. I try to have hope for humanity but with the clown we have in office as president currently, he's only encouraging hate even more in this country. Honestly, people from other countries either laugh at us, pity us, or a combination of both. A lot of them have realized both just how much of a loose cannon and imbecile our president is. Good grief, I hope

he doesn't get elected for a second term in office. Four

more years of him and we may never recover in many

aspects as a nation…

Let me say one more thing before I finally conclude

this rant, I love Virginia Beach with all of my heart. No

guy is going to stop me from continuing to spend time in a

place I love so dearly, no matter how awkward it may be at

times. The owner does like my parents and I, but he

certainly likes the money we put in his pockets. We've

been loyal guests here for several years now, he would

absolutely hate to lose regulars like us. I'm going to

continue to merely treat Jason like the hotel clerk he is and

nothing more. Gibson came around a bit today and I'm sure

that in due time, he'll be back to his normal self again. I

didn't get as many weird looks from him today and that

was definitely a start. Watching Jason stew over time will be satisfying enough revenge.

Chapter 10

Jason's POV

I've made several attempts already this evening to try to approach Emma but she's just not having it with me. Every time we make eye contact for even a mere couple of seconds, she immediately looks away and/or turns her back to me. It stings so badly but I know deep down that I deserve it. I made her hurt far more than she's hurting me. She has every right to ignore me like she is doing. I know I'm being selfish by trying to get her attention, but I just can't help it… I need to keep trying until I know for certain that there's no more potential for there ever being an "us." I take a deep breath and make my way out from behind the front desk yet again. Since there's no one else in the pool area besides Emma and the pool attendant on duty, I may have a chance this time.

Emma is sitting by the foot, splashing her feet around and just relaxing. My presence is going to ruin that vibe for her, but oh well… I clear my throat when I'm right behind her. She looks up at me and glares directly into my eyes. "What do you want?" I'm a bit taken aback by both her bluntness and her harsh tone of voice. "I-I wanted to apologize to you Emma. I've had a couple of days to process everything and I've come to realize that my reaction to that situation was completely uncalled for." She sighs. "I appreciate your attempt at an apology but I'm not quite ready to forgive you just yet Jason. Even if I was, I'd still just treat you like a worker and nothing more. I've also had a couple of days to process everything and deeply reflect. I've come to the realization that I crossed a line trying to even propose a relationship between us. For that, I'm sorry, but that's the only thing I apologize for."

I nod with my hands in my pant pockets, looking both pathetic and idiotic. The pool attendant gives me a glance of pity and I want to slide under the front desk right now, never to be seen again. "Emma, I honestly don't expect us to even be friends at this point. I know I messed up beyond belief and that some things just can't be fixed, our relationship/friendship with one another being one of them. If I really liked you as much as I had claimed I did, I wouldn't have hit on another girl within earshot of you. That was such a shitty thing for me to do. I know that if the shoe were on the other foot and you did that with another guy in my presence after claiming you liked me and only me, I'd go berserk." She nods. "Understandable. Well as much as I'm enjoying this chat, I'd like to go back to relaxing and pondering more on my life decisions. Also, someone is waiting for you to service their needs at the front desk."

I look up and see that she's indeed correct, someone is waiting for me at the front desk. I break into a sprint to attend to the guests' needs. I can practically feel her rolling her eyes at me behind my back. The guest needed some extra towels and wash cloths so they could take a shower. I went to the storage room down the hall to grab him some and he thanked me politely. Bless him for not being snippy with me. A snippy guest on top of a snippy Emma would probably push me over the edge right now. That interaction with Emma just a few minutes ago taught me enough to know that no matter how much I grovel to her, the most I'll receive from her is forgiveness eventually but despite that forgiveness, we'll never have what we had before. I don't want to live in a stage of denial and pretend like it's over forever, but that's the reality here, it's over. I had my chance with the most incredible woman I've ever known and I've ruined it beyond repair. I don't know if I'll ever be able to forgive myself for that... I don't think I even want to date anymore either... I'm just done.

Chapter 11

Emma's POV

 The interaction I had with Jason just now really was a testament to my strength. I was a total badass, truly. I'm so proud of myself. Jason absolutely deserves the cold shoulder, there's no way I'm going to go running back into his arms. This isn't the first time I've liked him but this is the only time I'll let him hurt me as badly as he did. He's probably going to shack up with that new housekeeping girl after he gets off tonight anyways. Chivalry and morals my ass... I continue to lounge by the pool for a little while longer, though to do some more thinking in private. It's nothing against my parents, it's just that I do my best thinking when I'm alone with my thoughts.

I can still feel Jason's gaze on me from the window that I see him standing near often that's by the front desk, but I refuse to stare at him. I think he got the message a bit though because he only comes in once more, not going anywhere near me in the process. He comes in to grab a spoon for his supper and keeps his gaze averted to the floor. I roll my eyes and snort just to get under his skin a bit further. I'm a very mature person but once in a while, I have my petty moments, this moment being one of those moments. When it gets close to the end of the pool time for tonight (pool closing time), I grab a towel off of the rack and begin the process of drying myself off so I don't streak water all across the lobby and down the hall to my room. I sit and air dry for a few minutes before finally leaving. I drop the towel in the hamper, wish the pool attendant a 'good night', and walk slowly back to my room (on purpose for dramatic effect).

Jason says my name once more. I stop in place but I don't turn around to look at him. "Emma, have a good night." I simply nod to the wall in front of me and head back to the room in silence. When I'm out of his sight, I smirk to myself. My performance this evening was a job well done if I may applaud myself. I tell my parents about it as soon as I enter the room and both of them nod in approval. My dad even breaks into applause for me. "I'm so freaking proud of you Emma! That was such a bold move that not many people have the courage to do. You sure put Jerkbag Jason in his place!" That statement causes me to giggle. "Jerkbag Jason, that's a good one. It sure has a catchy ring to it. Don't you think Mom?" She then laughs too. "It sure does. You know your father and some of zingers he comes out with. I have to say that that's one of his better ones as of recently." My dad playfully nudges her which leads to the two of them wrestling with each other affectionately in bed while I proceed to take a shower.

Chlorine lingering too long in my hair drives me crazy. I've made the mistake of falling asleep before after a swim and then regretting it when I wake up because after I shower, my hair is extra tangled and it hurts even more getting those tangles out. The warm water feels incredible on my skin as per usual. I wash away the smell of the chlorine and wind up smelling more like shampoo and soap, which is a much better smell. My hair is also tangle free as I brush it out after getting dressed. I put on a simple nightgown with underwear. I then brush my teeth and floss, sipping on wine with my mom while watching some reruns of Big Bang Theory together. That's a show that no matter how many times you watch each episode, it never gets old. I eventually find myself falling into a peaceful slumber, well before my mom even falls asleep for the night. I have pleasant dreams and even in my dreams come to terms with an evident truth, I'm a strong person and I can face future trips to Virginia Beach head on without cowering away in fear.

Chapter 12

Jason's POV

Time Skip... Two Days Later...

   Emma and her parents left yesterday morning to head back home and I've been in a funk ever since, even more so than before. I'm really coming to regret my actions but what I regret even more is knowing that I can't fix this. Throughout my entire life, I've been superb at problem solving but when it comes to repairing even a friendship with Emma, I'm realizing it's beyond repair. She gave me the coldest gaze when she spoke to me for that brief moment last night. If looks could kill, hers easily could have sliced my heart open. The new pool attendant/housekeeper is working on pool duty tonight and

I'm sick to my stomach. Looking at her actually makes me want to upchuck.

She comes out from time to time, frowning at my dismay towards her. "Jason, what's wrong? Clearly my presence is bothering you." I sigh and run a hand through my hair, one of my most prominent stress habits. "I've got to be honest, your presence is bothering me tonight but it isn't really your fault. You were scheduled to work the pool tonight and you're doing your job. I just made a really dumb decision and I'm kicking myself in the ass for it." She tilts her head in confusion. "And it somehow involves me?" "Yes, it does. You were being very flirty with me the other day and I was weak enough to succumb to yet another female co-worker of mine coming onto me. It was a mistake, nothing can happen between us."

Her eyes quickly water and her lip quivers, making me feel even shittier than I already do. "I'm sorry to be harsh but I have to be honest. There was a girl that I really like... I mean liked. I've wanted to get together with her for a long time and when I finally had a proper chance, I blew it. I'm nowhere near ready to jump back into the dating game with anyone." She stays silent for a minute before speaking again. "It's that Emma girl, isn't it?" At the mention of Emma, my heart dips into my stomach, more sadness setting in. She's got me, I can't weasel my way out of this one. I need to be honest and tell the truth. I look her directly in the eyes and say "Yes, it is." She whimpers and goes back into the pool area, not wanting to say anything else to me. She only comes out when she asks me to cover for her once so she that can use the bathroom.

I'm so frustrated with myself, I hurt everyone I come in contact with. I of all people don't deserve to be throwing myself a pity party, but I'm throwing myself one anyway. I don't think I deserve to be with anyone… I can't bear the thought of hurting another woman, especially one as incredible as Emma. Oh let's face it, there will never be another Emma. I'd be lucky to even find someone half as decent as she is. I'm a monster, an absolute monster. Emma is going to put me in the same category as that other asshole she dated that also works her, the head of maintenance. Good grief, I can't stand that guy. Him and I often go toe to toe and Gibson has to help settle our disagreements. Bless Gibson for doing so but I can tell that he gets sick of having to do so. I get through the rest of my shift in one piece but by the time I get to my car after locking up and clocking out for the night, I break down yet again in my car.

Emma probably isn't giving me a single thought. She's probably back to work and ranting to her co-workers and friends about how lousy of a guy I am. I know I certainly would if I were in her shoes. I take my time to let all of my feelings out and calm down a bit before I begin my trek home. There's very little traffic on the road at this time of night but I want to be an semi-decent frame of mind when I'm behind the wheel. Driving while extremely emotional doesn't tend to end well for anyone involved.

Emma's POV

That night...

I'm downing a glass of chardonnay with my mom after a long work day. I'm still trying to get over Jason. I've only gotten teary eyed twice today, which is a record low thus far. My mom and I are reflecting on the entire situation, everything from the harassment aspects from the fellow hotel guest to Jason's handling of it. My mother and I are both in agreement that he handled the situation poorly. He bluffed far too much for our liking. It's ironic how a man can often receive all of the glory and a woman is the one who is shamed for simply being herself. A woman should be able to wear a nice outfit and walk around the neighborhood in peace without having to face harassment from anyone. Jason's negative reaction that night has brought out several of my insecurities that I thought I had buried down ... but apparently not.

I want to be able to get back to a place again eventually where for the most part, I'm content with myself as a person. I want to be able to feel comfortable wearing cute outfits in public, not panicking because I'm showing a little tummy and/or a little cleavage. Drinking a bit with my mom and pouring my heart out is actually helping me though, even just a little. My dad chips in from time to time but he's pretty tired so I don't expect him to blab as much as my mom and I are. My parents are truly my best friends, I don't know what I'd do without them. Even at twenty five years old, I depend on them a lot for support, especially moral support.

Chapter 13

Emma's POV

Time Skip... About Two Months Later...

It's been about two months since I've last been to the hotel in Virginia Beach. I've missed it a lot but yet the break was much needed, did wonders for my mental state. Being away from Virginia Beach for a bit really helped me get over Jason for good. If I had continued to have back to back stays at the hotel, my feelings for Jason would have lingered even longer, which would have been brutal for my mental/emotional health. My feelings for him are finally gone completely though. I don't hate him anymore, I just deeply dislike him. I'm actually on my way to the hotel for the first time since that fateful stay, the stay that changed everything between us. I take a series of deep breaths, especially as I pull into the parking lot. My mom couldn't come along for this trip, but thankfully my dad was still able to tag along. It's kind of nice because my dad and I haven't had any one on one quality time together in quite a while. It should be a great weekend, well hopefully…

My dad did the driving down here because I was a little nervous too and because I also had a lot on my mind. I'll do the rest of the driving down here though. I get out of the car first and head inside to check in. Jason shoots straight up out of his chair at the sight of me heading towards him. He fidgets with his tie and awkwardly stands behind the front desk. "Emma." I nod. "Jason. I'm here to check in." He nods back. "Just you and your Dad this time?" "Yup." He sighs and types a few things into the computer before activating the card reader so I can pay for this stay. It takes me three times to get the machine to read the chip in my debit card successfully, but it does go through on the third try. The bill isn't too expensive because the off season deals have officially begun. He then sanitizes some room keys, puts them in an envelope, and hands them over to me. To spite me, he doesn't volunteer to carry any of our bags. I have to make two trips to carry everything to the room and then a third in order to tell my dad to come inside. He makes sure to lock the car because someone attempted to break into the car last month to steal both his medication stored in his pill box and some money.

When everything is brought into the room, I begin the process of unpacking and getting settled. Upon entering the bathroom, I notice that the shower bench and bars aren't in there for my dad and I groan. Great, I have to go deal with Jason yet again. I sigh aloud. "Dad, I have to go bother Jason for the shower bench and bars. We also could use some extra towels. I'll be right back." He nods. "Take your time." I put the 'do not disturb' sign up on the door so no one bothers him. I patiently wait for Jason to check in another guest before asking him for the essential items that we need. He practically throws the towels at me but thankfully doesn't throw the shower bench or bars at me a few minutes later. In fact, he actually installs the bars and puts in the bench himself. I guess a small part of him feels for my elderly dad. He then looks me over strangely for a moment before leaving the room.

I close the door and roll my eyes. "Dad, he's something else. I'm convinced that he evolves into a more stranger being each and every day." My dad snorts. "I agree with you darling but there's one more thing I'd like to add to that statement, which is he's a guy who knows that he has lost the best thing that ever could have happened to him when it comes to genuine love." I get tear eyed instantly. My dad is often tough and macho, but he also has a sweet, soft side too. I bend down to give him a gentle hug. "Thank you Dad, I needed to hear that. Thank you, I love you. Getting over Jason was one of the hardest things I've ever had to do in my life but yet I somehow managed to do so against all odds." He hugs me back and kisses me on the forehead. "I'm so proud of you Emma and I love you too, so very much."

We both opt out of going to the pool area tonight and have a movie night for a change. I'm a massive Marvel fan and Avengers: Age of Ultron happens to be playing one of the movie channels. My dad is really into it and is beginning to see why I'm so obsessed with this franchise, both with the comics and the movies/shows within the Marvel Universe also known as the Marvel Cinematic Universe. Before bed though, I call my Mom to check in on her for a few minutes. She's doing just fine and urges us not to worry about her. She's kind of happy to have some time alone for a change. It's nothing personal, she just doesn't get much alone time. I'm not offended because I can relate to that all too well. I end up having the best night's sleep I've had in months during the night. I hope the rest of the weekend goes smoothly too.

Chapter 14

Jason's POV

The next evening...

I didn't see much of Emma and her father last night and I think I know why, she doesn't want to deal with me unless she has to. In simple terms, she's avoiding me. Emma and her father are heading directly towards the pool area. She avoids eye contact with me as she opens the door and helps her father enter it. She then glares at me for a second before walking away. I roll my eyes. Two can play at this game Emma, just you wait. I roll up the sleeves of my shirt and march in there not too far behind her. "Emma, is this necessary?" She sits up straight in her chair. "Jason, do you need something or are you just trying to pick a bone with me?"

I put my hands on my hips and shoot a glance at the pool attendant to go take that bathroom break she's been whining to me about wanting to take for nearly an hour now. She takes heed of my warning and goes to use the bathroom. "I've made several attempts to be civil with you and you're being nothing but disrespectful towards me Emma." She laughs quite bitterly. "You've got to be kidding me Jason! You didn't take my feelings into account on that fateful night a few months ago and you ignored every single one of my three attempts to make amends. Now that the shoe is on the other foot and I'm giving you the same negative treatment you gave me, it's just eating you alive. That's not my fault nor is it my problem." Her father gives me a dirty look and looks as though he may begin telling me off pretty soon. I should probably shut my big mouth but I just can't seem to do so.

"Emma, don't make me banish you from my life altogether." She snorts. "Your actions made that clear three months ago Jason. I've gotten past it. I'm over it, I'm over you. You should get back to doing your job. Go nose into the business of other guests, I'm not the only guest here to worry about. The more you obsess over me, the more pathetic it makes you look as a person." Her father nods in agreement. "You heard her Jason, scram." My jaw is absolutely slack. I try to force my feet to move but they won't, they're frozen in place. Emma studies me carefully and then begins taunting me. "What's wrong Jason? Is your anxiety kicking in? Normally I'm very understanding about that sort of thing but when someone mocks and belittles me for having that exact condition, I find it difficult to feel sympathetic towards that individual." She shrugs her shoulders. "Sorry."

I look like an absolute fool. I'm still frozen in place and even Emma's father doesn't feel any sympathy for me. As I continue to stand there until the pool attendant comes back from the bathroom, I come to yet another revelation. Not only is Emma completely done with me, but not even her parents feel anything but resentment towards me. They're a little more civil to me than Emma is but at the end of the day, they'll always support Emma through and through. Emma's their daughter after all, I'm nothing to them. I then go back to manning the desk, for once super grateful for the extreme rush of guests needing assistance checking in, carrying luggage up to their rooms, and other inquiries relating to the hotel. I don't dare glance in Emma and/or her father's direction again for the rest of the evening. I simply lock up the pool area behind them at closing time since they stayed until the very last minute.

The two of them quietly head back to their room in silence. Once they're away from me, they begin conversing with each other again. I hear voices echo off of the walls for a minute before they finally enter their room, closing the door behind them. I'm certain Emma put the 'do not disturb' sign up on the door and locked it, bolting it shut too. No time to dwell on her any further tonight, I have yet another rush of customers to attend to. Work keeps me busy enough for the last hour or so of my shift that I don't have another mental episode, even after I clock out and get in my car to drive home.

Chapter 15

Emma's POV

Time Skip... Two Months Later...

I've done a lot of deep thinking over the last couple of months. During this period of time, I returned twice more to the hotel and ignored Jason altogether during both stays. He finally got the memo to give me my space thankfully. I don't want to be petty anymore though. At first it was fun but now it's just mentally exhausting. I just want him to know that I've moved on completely, which is the truth. I have moved on from Jason. I don't have feelings for anyone else but I am finally open to the prospect of dating someone other than Jason down the road. I just don't want to waste any more time from here on out.

On a positive note, I did get promoted at work recently. I also got a decent raise too and that has made me gain my confidence back in my abilities. My bosses treat me with respect, value me as a worker, and communicate with me regularly. I'm sitting at home soaking my feet in epsom salts to ease my aching feet a bit. I've been on my feet all day today. I have my phone in my lap and I'm thinking about making a call that I'm finally ready to make. I scroll through my contacts to find the hotel's main number. Once I do, I press dial and anxiously wait for it to ring. Someone picks up on the fourth ring... and of course it's Jason. I expected this but I'm still anxious. "Good evening, this is the *insert hotel name here*." "Jason, it's Emma." A moment of silence passes before he speaks again. He awkwardly clears his throat and I roll my eyes.

"Emma, are you calling to make a reservation?" "No, I'm not." "What are you calling for then?" "I'm calling to say that I forgive you for hurting me. I'm done being petty, I'm done embarrassing you. I apologize for being petty, I promise you that it's over." "W-Well, I, uh, appreciate the apology. I apologize for not respecting your wishes of giving you space. You are a valued guest here as is your family. I don't want to be the reason all of you stop coming here. I don't want to be the cause of tainting special memories of a place you've come to love." "I forgive you Jason. We're both adults. As long as we think with our minds rather than letting our hearts over take us, things should be fine. That's all I have to say. Bye Jason." He takes a shaky breath. "Bye Emma." I hang up and sit back in my chair, taking a moment to absorb the conversation we just had.

I think that both of us have shown some personal growth in how we've begun to slowly move on from each other. We had our shot to try to be an item but it's over now as I've started multiple times now. Jason and I aren't meant to be together and that's okay. It may have taken me a few months to properly accept that, but it's better late than never, right? I certainly think so. I meant what I said over the phone though, I really have forgiven Jason for his past actions. What I do hope for though is that he doesn't hurt another woman as badly as he did me. I hope he learned a valuable lesson from that experience and treats other women that he becomes friends with and/or starts dating with more respect.

Jason's POV

I just received a surprise phone call from Emma and it shook me up a bit. I have to say it went pretty well though all things considered. She promised to stop throwing jabs at me which I do appreciate. Every time she threw a jab

my way, it reminded me of how badly I screwed up.

Hurting Emma is always going to be one of my biggest

regrets but recently, I finally started to be able to look at

myself again in the mirror and not to want to vomit at the

sight of my reflection staring back at me. I too have

forgiven Emma but in addition to forgiving her, I finally

have begun to forgive myself. I learned a valuable lesson

out of this experience. I've learned that I never want to hurt

another woman so terribly, especially such an incredible

one like Emma ever again.

I've also learned that I need to take some time to work

on my own issues before I can take on someone else's full

time. I'm not the man that I want to be and I want to

achieve the goal of becoming a better man before I even

consider the prospect of dating again. Emma will always

be in the back of my mind but I need to continue moving

forward. I can't stop living my life because one woman stopped having feelings for me. We're not meant to be and it's time for me to accept that.

Chapter 16

Jason's POV

 Major Time Skip... A Year Later...

    Emma is twenty six now, nearing twenty seven pretty soon while I just turned forty two last week. Time is flying and both of us are getting older. You're probably wondering if the two of us even speak to each other anymore. The answer is not really. We're cordial to each other when we do speak but our conversations never exceed small talk about the weather, the hotel, etc. Speaking of Emma, she dashes down the stairs rather quickly in a black cocktail style dress with a matching clutch and heels to go with it. My heart sinks a bit as I quickly realize that she's going out on a date. She came down here alone this time around and she certainly didn't get dressed up that fancy for herself. She waits a few minutes for a cab to arrive outside but I don't bother to approach her. I don't want to know the details, it'll just shatter me even further.

I know, I know, it's been over a year now. I should have at least begun to move on, but the truth is I haven't. I've been approached by a couple of decent women to go out on dates but every time I'd talk to them, my mind would drift back to Emma. When she gets into the cab and rides off to wherever she's meeting her date, I shed the tears that have built up inside of me. They come flowing out like a river. It's so bad that Gibson actually hears my muffled sobs from his apartment in the back and he comes out to check on me. He sits down beside me, comforting me as I let all of my emotions out. He even throws away my snot filled tissues afterwards. "Jason, can I give you some advice?" I nod while still sniffling.

Gibson looks me directly in the eyes with a serious expression on his face, which is how I know that he's going to speak the whole truth and nothing but the truth. "Jason, there's a part of her that still cares about you. She stills calls the hotel when you're not on duty from time to time and even asks for you. While she still cares about your well-being and you continuing to keep your position as assistant manager, you need to begin to put Emma in your rearview mirror. I'm saying this both as your supervisor and as a friend. Dwelling over Emma like this and over your past mistakes isn't going to get you anywhere but having grey hairs several years earlier than expected. Emma has moved on, she's going out on a date tonight with a guy she's been speaking to for about three months who lives in the area. They seem to get along quite well and there's potential for a relationship there. You need to respect that."

I nod along but don't say anything so he continues to do so for me. "Yes Jason, what you did was lousy. Your actions were terrible and you not bothering to even attempt to understand Emma's anxiety was a low blow both to her and even to me. That girl has the biggest heart of any young lady I've ever met. She didn't deserve to have experienced as much pain as you attributed to her last summer. Despite that though, it's well in the past now. You should move on too, begin to find some happiness again. Whether it be going out on a date with a new person like

Emma is or just simply picking up a new hobby or interest. Are you willing to at least try Jason?" I sigh. "I'm not even remotely ready to date anyone else in the near future, but I do like the sound of picking up a new hobby/interest in my spare time. I'd like to get into biking more."

Gibson gives me a small smile. "There you go Jason, that's a good start. Go to a bike store when you can, pick out a nice bike, and take it out for a spin. Having the ocean basically in our backyard has its perks. Am I right?" I crack a tired smile. "Yeah you're right, thank you Gibson. I really needed this talk tonight." He pats me on the back. "Anytime. Are you hungry? I can whip you up something. My wife has leftover meatloaf and steamers." My stomach rumbles, revealing my starvation to him. "I could go for some meatloaf, if it isn't too much trouble that is. I know you're tired, you worked an eight hour shift earlier." "Nonsense. Give me about ten minutes and I'll have some meatloaf for you." "Thank you Gibson." He nods and comes back with a plate full of meatloaf as promised ten minutes later. I gobble the meatloaf in a piggish manner and Gibson comes out a little while later to take the plate and utensils back to wash them.

I'm extremely grateful for Gibson tonight, more so than ever before. It's so rare for someone to actually notice how much a person is hurting inside these days, it's even rarer for them to take the time to comfort that person and offer up much needed words of wisdom. He even made me dinner on top of it. I'll never forget Gibson's kind gestures from tonight and that's a promise. I'm going to purchase a new bike on my day off on Thursday and I'm going to go biking. I'm going to feel the breeze whipping my hair around, absorb the smell of the ocean, and calm my ever racing heart by listening to the waves crash against the shore. I'm also going to lose a few pounds in the process and get some much needed exercise. This is the beginning of a new journey for me and I can't wait to see where it takes me.

Chapter 17

Emma's POV

Later that evening...

I end up coming back from my date about two hours early because it was such a disaster. Jason is still working the front desk and I'm trying to avoid eye contact with him at all costs. It's so obvious that he knew I was going out on a date and I really don't want to be grilled about it, especially not by him. I don't need any more awkwardness between us. I'm so sick of the heels that I'm wearing that once I get near the entrance, I take them off and simply walk in my peds/shoe inserts instead. As I approach my room, I can feel someone's presence behind me... and it's Jason. Greeeeaaatttt... *Note my sarcasm*

"Look Jason, I'm not really in the mood to converse right now, especially not about my personal business and/or my love life." He sighs. "I know, I just wanted to make sure you were okay is all." I sigh back. "I'm fine, just tired. It's been a long day. I'd like to go to my room and relax. Is that okay with you?" He nods and steps aside, allowing me to enter my room. He then enters the room because my exhausted self happened to forget to close the door behind me. "Jason, what on Earth are you doing? You don't come into my room unless I need something to be fixed or a hotel related service. This is extremely unprofessional and I'm respectfully asking you to leave my room."

Jason nods and begins to leave but hesitates before getting back to the door. "I know I fucked things up between us beyond repair. I know it's over between us, whatever we could have been is no more. I'm finally beginning to accept that as I told you once before, I just regret treating you as lousy as I did. I'm frustrated that you went out on a date with someone else, but yet I'm frustrated that the date didn't go well for you because you deserve the very best. Again, I apologize from the bottom of my heart for not being able to give my very best to you. I've also realized that I do indeed have a lot of issues to work through, some even including mental and emotional issues. I can't be a decent man to a woman if I don't begin to find ways to overcome and/or cope with these issues. I hope that someday you find someone who can give you everything you deserve and then some."

I give him a tired smile. "Thank you again for the apology Jason. I appreciate it. I hope you're able to overcome and/or come to cope with your issues in due time. I hope you find happiness and peace, whether it be with a new partner down the road and/or a new passion. I don't want to get any deeper than this because I can't dive into the past with you any longer. It's too mentally exhausting." He nods. "I understand Emma." Without another word, he finally leaves the room and closes the door behind him. I lock and bolt it shut before flopping down onto my bed. I'm about to have a deep thinking session myself.

Tonight's date was one of the worst dates I've had in a long time. We had dinner at a Greek restaurant on the main beach strip. Wayne (the guy I went out on a date with) was such a drag. I'm not the most exciting person myself but I don't exactly get thrills out of talking about the best kind of electrical sockets to plug extension cords into... for an hour straight. I wish I was exaggerating about that but I'm not. Wayne also doesn't like to drink which is absolutely valid but yet he shamed me for having ONE glass of wine, just one. Way to be a hypocrite dude. Seriously though, I don't think I want to go out on another date for a long time. I really need to deeper evaluate what I'm looking for in a partner and what I need to avoid at all costs. The main challenge is that you don't always know the cons of a potential partner until you meet them in person. *Sighs*

I've finally properly forgiven Jason for hurting me so badly as you already know but the more he shows his face and tries to get into my business (whether it be on purpose or by accident), I'll be moving backwards rather than forwards, which is something I can't afford to be doing. Jason preaches about wanting peace but guess what, I want to find some peace too. I'm worthy of finding peace just as much as he is.

Epilogue

Writer's POV

Time Skip... A Year Later...

Jason and Emma have both moved on and gone their separate ways. Both of them have had their temptations to speak to each other beyond the small talk one more than one occasion but at the end of the day, neither one of them let common sense get the best of them thankfully. Neither one of them is a bad person, they're just bad together. Separately, both of them do just fine though. Does that make sense? I think it does, I've heard that expression before from my very own parents. Jason has stuck with his vow of biking on a regular basis and keeping up with his fitness regimen since he is fast approaching middle age. He isn't dating anyone else still after all of this time. He's committed to his work and hobbies, also tending to his mother too.

Emma also has been focusing more on her career, to the point where she has worked her way up to management level. She got the promotion last month and has been doing a remarkable job, often receiving praise from her higher ups about her work ethic. Emma has always been a passionate person, going big or going home when it comes to things and people that she loves most. Her parents are still in good health despite continuing to age and she's grateful for them each and every day. Emma too hasn't dived into any new relationships. She did try going out with someone a couple months ago but it didn't work out beyond the first date. Her and the guy she went out with did get along quite well though and agreed to stay friends. He kept his word because he reaches out at least twice a week to chat with her and check on her well-being (and vice versa of course). That's very rare these days so always appreciate people like that, people who can accept no for an answer when romance doesn't work out but yet they still value enough to want to be your friend.

Overall, things are going quite well for both Emma and Jason. While the tale of their romance that could have been is over completely, neither one of them has stopped living their lives. As difficult as it may be to accept, sometimes people aren't meant to be as a couple. It often

takes them a long time to accept that evident truth too.

Some things are meant to come into your life, but just

aren't meant to stay. The trials and errors of Emma and

Jason are proof of that.

THE END

Author's Note

I hope that you all enjoyed reading this book as much as I

enjoyed writing it. Just a friendly reminder though that

this book is self-published and self-edited by yours truly. :)

Feel free to add/follow me on my following social media accounts/apps:

Twitter: @iamsporty657

Snapchat: marygotswagg657

Youtube: iamsporty657/ Mary Whitney

Wattpad: iamsporty657

TikTok: marygotswagg657

 All of my other books can be purchased on Amazon as well, including my bestsellers such as 'Surviving A Modern Pandemic', 'Bettering Myself', and 'Danger Zone'. Feel free to reach out to me if you want a complete list of all of my books and I'll happily respond back with one. ☺ -Mary

28-Day Diabetes Weight Loss Plan

Delicious and Nutritious Meals to Help You Reach Your Goals

John M. Flint